Once upon a time ...

Story & illustrations by:
Iris B. Willinger

www.irisbwillinger.com

©2022 All Rights Reserved

Dubi was a curious, young bear - but he was an orphan - so lived alone in a very large forest. He loved to sing and whistle all day long. Whistling, he had learnt from the birds, and singing from his mother.
Every winter he hibernated - as bears do.

He had never experienced a real winter, as he was usually asleep. Dubi had never seen snowflakes either, but the animals told him it was something quite magical.

He heard that snowflakes were like soft stars falling from the sky; thousands and thousands of them. They would turn the ground into a diamond sparkling blanket.

Dubi decided that this year, he would not hibernate but find out where snowflakes came from.

Soon, the days grew shorter, and one November evening it started to snow. Dubi just stood there staring at the sky.

The animals had been right - it WAS magical!

In no time there was a white blanket on everything. He licked a few snowflakes off his paw. They were cold and tasty. His winter fur was so thick, he did not mind the cold, and so fell asleep under the starry sky, snoring happily.

The next morning the winter sun tickled his nose and he woke up with a sneeze. HAAAAATCHHUUUU!!! His eyes grew bigger.

All around him was a glistening winter wonderland. He walked to the river and watched the iceflowers around the stones. It was so beautiful, he made up a little melody.

A curious fox heard him and came closer.

"Hi, I am Finna. You have a very lovely voice."
"Hello, I am Dubi ... the singing bear," Dubi replied a bit shy. See, he was a solitary bear and not used to company.
"Nice to meet you, Dubi. Why are you not hibernating? You are a bear after all?"

Finna's whiskers twitched with curiosity.

Snow is here, snow is there
Snowflakes falling everywhere
Winter, winter is finally here
wish that it could stay all year!

She scratched her head confused; Finna was usually a clever fox.

Dubi explained: "I should sleep in my cave now, but I really want to know where snowflakes come from. Do you know?"

Finna looked up at the sky and wrinkled her snout.
"No, I don't know where they come from. They just fall from the sky. I never thought about why. But now you made me curious. I think there is someone in the Northlands who might know."

Dubi took a handful of snow and smiled at the fox.
"Do you want to come with me on an adventure? We could solve the snowflake mystery! It would be nice to have company."

"Oh, that sounds exciting, yes! I would like that! I know the forest well in winter and it's always more fun if you have good company."
Finna did not tell him that she was quite lonely during the winter, and missed someone to talk to.

After a long day walking they were both hungry and decided to take a rest. They had come to a lovely Oak forest where they met a badger. He was digging for some juicy roots and grub.

"Hi, I am Finna and this is Dubi. Can you tell us where snowflakes come from, please? We have asked many animals already, but nobody seems to know."

The badger grunted and looked surprised at the newcomers. "You want to know where snowflakes come from? That's easy! From the sky of course. There, mystery solved!"

"Oh, we know they fall from the sky but who makes them and where? It's a mystery?"

The badger looked up and scratched his fur: "Well, that IS a good question. I never did think of that. Would you mind if I joined you," he asked very excited. "Oh, and my name is Mr. Schnutz, pleased to meet you."

He took a little bow.

Finna clapped her paws. "That's great, now we are three!"

On their way north, they found a bird hopping on the ground.
It was an injured magpie who had a sprained wing. They stopped and helped the bird on Dubi's back, so it could recover.

"Thank you so much! I do not wknow what I would have done without you. I am Moxi."
She was a chatty bird, and knew about the Northlands. They told her about the snowflake mystery and Moxi said: "I think there is a Snowfairy in the Northlands. If we reach her, she might be able to help us. But we need to go through the Iceforest... a dangerous place."

They did not like the sound of that, but were too tired to worry. Dubi looked for a suitable shelter and they fell asleep instantly.

The next moring brought bright sunshine. They were all rested and made new tracks in the fresh fallen snow.

Moxi tried to flutter, but her wing still hurt so she stayed on Dubi's back. He did not mind; she was feather light.
The magpie turned to the others.
"When I flew around last week, I saw the castle of the Snowfairy in the Northlands. If we ever want to find out where snowflakes come from, she is the one who knows. But, but, but ...," she looked around nervously and whispered: "there are ghosts in the Iceforest!"

Dubi stopped suddenly and Mr. Schnutz and Finna ran into him, tumbling backwards into the deep snow.
"Ghosts? That sounds very scary!"
The bear looked at the others as they seemed frightened too. Then Mr. Schnutz remembered something.
"I know of a deer. It has snow magic and might be able to help us. Perhaps we could ask if it could guide us through the Iceforest?"

Finna and Moxi nodded.
"That is a splendid idea Mr. Schnutz. Can you take us to her?"
"Yes I can indeed." So, onwards they stomped through the snow.

When they reached the bottom of the valley it was late afternoon and the sun was low. Suddenly it all went very quiet around them, as if the whole forest was holding its breath.

They stood very still as a tall animal on very long legs came towards them. It was the most beautiful creature they had ever seen and was surrounded by a magical light.
The deer tilted its head and smiled: "Hello, welcome to my forest. You must have come a long way."

Finna bowed as she thought it was the proper thing to do.
"We have come a long way indeed. See, we want to solve a mystery."
"Oh, a mystery? That sounds exciting."
"We want to know where snowflakes come from, and need to get through the Iceforest to reach the Snowfairy. Could you help us, please?"
The deer was quiet for a long while, and looked at each of them.

Suddenly it smiled: "I would be glad to help you, but first…"

The deer scratched the snow and mumbled something. Suddenly the snow started to dance and whirl towards Moxi and surrounded the bird in a flurry cloud and magical sparkles landed on her wing.
"Oh, look, my wing is ok again!"
Moxi fluttered and was delighted. "Thank you so much!"
"Look, look ... I can fly again!"
And she took off into the tops of the trees laughing.

The deer called Moxi back and said to them: "Tonight is a special night - it's Christmas Eve - so we must celebrate and eat. It is getting dark soon, so you can stay with me. We shall head to the Iceforest early tomorrow and well rested."

All agreed, and were glad they had such a lovely new guide. They didn't need any gifts, they had already received the greatest one of all: Friendship!

Sitting around a tree full of lights, Dubi sang his winter song until it was time to sleep. "My first Christmas ever ... thank you all!"

The next morning they set off early and made good time. But once they arrived at the Iceforest, within seconds, they no longer saw the path as thick fog had drifted in suddenly. The deer stopped, closed its eyes and mumbled something, stomping its hoof. Slowly, the snow in front of them started to light up - like a trail of fairy lights. They could finally walk on to just wanted to get out of this spooky place.

In the trees a jingling sound grew louder. "What is that!" Moxi croaked.

"The trees sing of a time, when this was still a lovely forest. It was full of animals and wildflowers. This was before it was cursed by a magician. See, the magician's daughter went out onto the lake on the ice - to help an animal - and she fell through the ice. The magician was so heartbroken and angry, he cursed the whole forest to be forever covered in ice. Only a few winter ghosts are still haunting it today, trying to lure wanderers onto the lake. The magician himself disappeared a long time ago; nobody knows what happened to him."

They were high in the mountains when night fell, and they had finally reached the end of the Iceforest.
Mr. Schnutz scuttled off on his little badger legs to collect sticks and then made a fire with some flint stones he found. He was a very resourceful friend. Soon, the bright flames warmed them nicely. They were all half frozen after their climb.

The fog had lifted and a beautiful and clear night sky appeared. They even saw a shooting star.

"Quick, quick ... make a wish!"
Moxi fluttered on a rock and pointed upwards.
"Such a beautiful night and we are all safe now.
Finna started counting: "One, two, three, four ..."

The others laughed out loud. "Finna, you'll never finish counting the stars, there are too many of them. Go to sleep!"
They all curled up under an old pine tree around the fire.

Each had made a wish.
But as wishes go, you can't tell anyone.

For two more days they hiked north and saw many beautiful things on the way, like a frozen waterfall with juicy berry bushes.

Finally, they could see the gates of the Snowfairy's castle in the distance. Moxi and Mr. Schnutz did a little happy-dance, and they all laughed as it looked rather silly. When they stood at the gates, they could hear lovely bells announcing their arrival.

The doors opened and there was such a flurry of snow, they could not see anything. Once the snowflakes settled, there, right in front of them, stood the Snowfairy. She was surrounded by a group of small elves that giggled. Had they never seen a bear, a fox, a badger, a deer or a magpie.

"Thank you for welcoming us," Dubi said politely. The Snowfairy smiled: "Please, come in, come in! We rarely have guests, so this is a lovely surprise. You all look very hungry."

The Snowfairy waved them inside. Dubi blushed as his tummy was rumbling quite loud.

After they were fed a delicious meal, Dubi asked the Snowfairy: "We wanted to find out where snowflakes come from. Do you know who makes them?"

The Snowfairy laughed: "But of course I do! They are made right here and then distributed by my brother, the cloud elf, all over the world."

She led them into a large workshop and there were thousands of elves crafting snowflakes, which were then packed and shipped off. It was
all very efficient.

Dubi looked around and clapped his hands: "Ha, now we have solved the mystery of the snowflakes!"

They went back to the dining hall where Dubi started to sing for them.

When they finally got tired and rolled up to sleep, the Snowfairy smiled and sprinkled glittering snowflakes on all of them, and disappeared quietly through a doorway.

The next morning, Dubi woke up slowly. A little confused, he stretched himself, looked around and blinked. But what was that? He was in his own forest, only a short distance from his cave and... he was alone.

He could not have dreamt all this, could he? Dubi felt a little itch on his back and pulled a small feather from his fur. It was Moxi's.
But where were they? The Snowfairy must have something to do with this. He leaned on a tree and was suddenlt very sad, so started picking some berries, as he always got hungry when he was nervous.

Suddenly there was giggling and then loud laughter echoing from behind a snowhill. Slowly, all his friends' heads appeared over a snow-drift: first Finna, then Mr. Schnutz, then Moxi and the deer.

Dubi was so glad to see them. He started a snowball fight, and the others joined in.
When they had enough of playing, everyone gathered for breakfast, and they talked about the adventures of the past days.

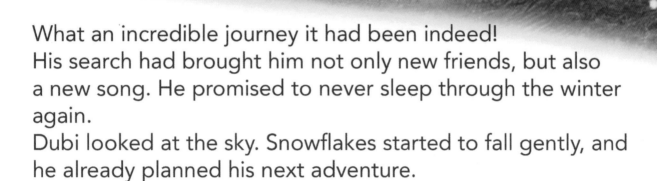

What an incredible journey it had been indeed!
His search had brought him not only new friends, but also
a new song. He promised to never sleep through the winter
again.
Dubi looked at the sky. Snowflakes started to fall gently, and
he already planned his next adventure.

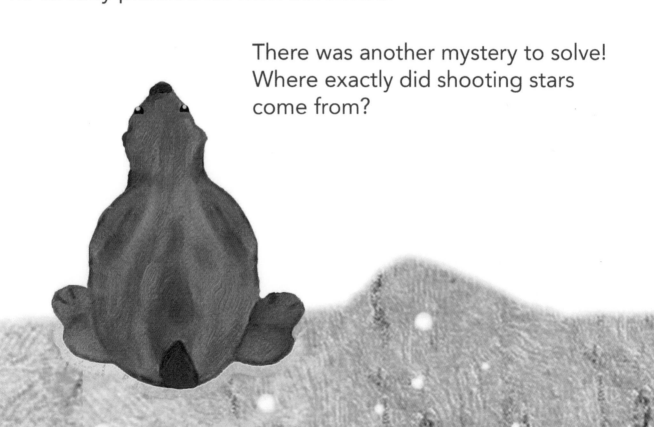

There was another mystery to solve!
Where exactly did shooting stars
come from?

Find out more about the
author & illustrator, and
get a preview of upcoming books:

www.irisbwillinger.com

Printed in Great Britain
by Amazon

31867755R00018